Otto was a penguin chick. He lived on his father's feet
at the bottom of the world.

South
America

Africa

Antarctica

Antarctica

The most southern region of the world,
with the coldest temperatures.
There is no sunlight for four months
of the year; it is only night. It is one of
the harshest places on planet Earth,
but it is where emperor penguins live.

EGMONT

We bring stories to life

This edition first published 2009 by
Egmont UK Limited, 239 Kensington High Street, London W8 6SA
First published 1972 by Methuen & Co. Ltd
Text copyright © The Estate of Jill Tomlinson 1972
Abridgement by permission of the Estate
Illustrations © Paul Howard 2009
Paul Howard has asserted his moral rights
A CIP catalogue record for this title is available from the British Library
All rights reserved.

ISBN 978 1 4052 3040 7 (hb)
ISBN 978 1 4052 3041 4 (pb)

1 3 5 7 9 10 8 6 4 2
Printed and bound in Singapore

For David, who has been to the Antarctic,
his wife Pat, and the boys, James, Peter
and Matthew, and of course Claudius
J.T.

For James
P.H.

The Penguin who Wanted to Find Out

words by
Jill Tomlinson

illustrated by
Paul Howard

EGMONT

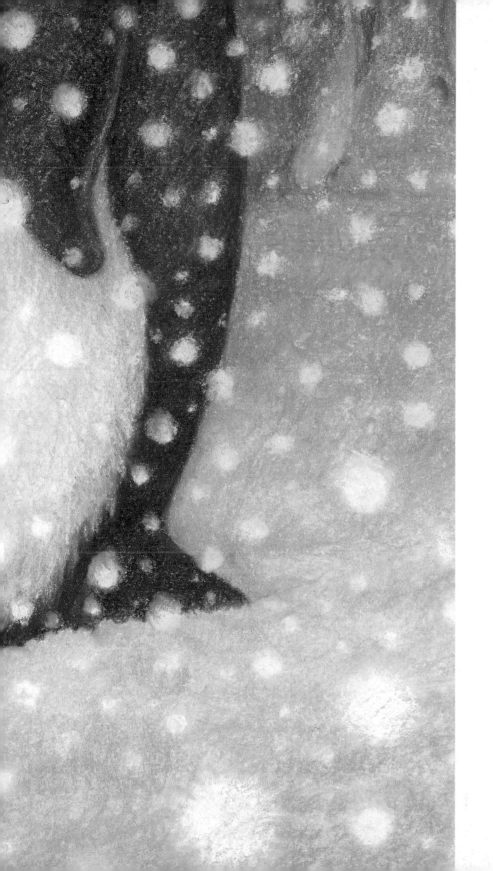

'How do you know we're
at the bottom of the world?'
Otto asked his friend, Leo.
'Your father told my father,'
said Leo. 'Your father
knows everything.'

Otto thought for a moment.
Then he shouted up at Claudius,
'Dad, there are lots of things
I want to know about.
Please talk to me!'

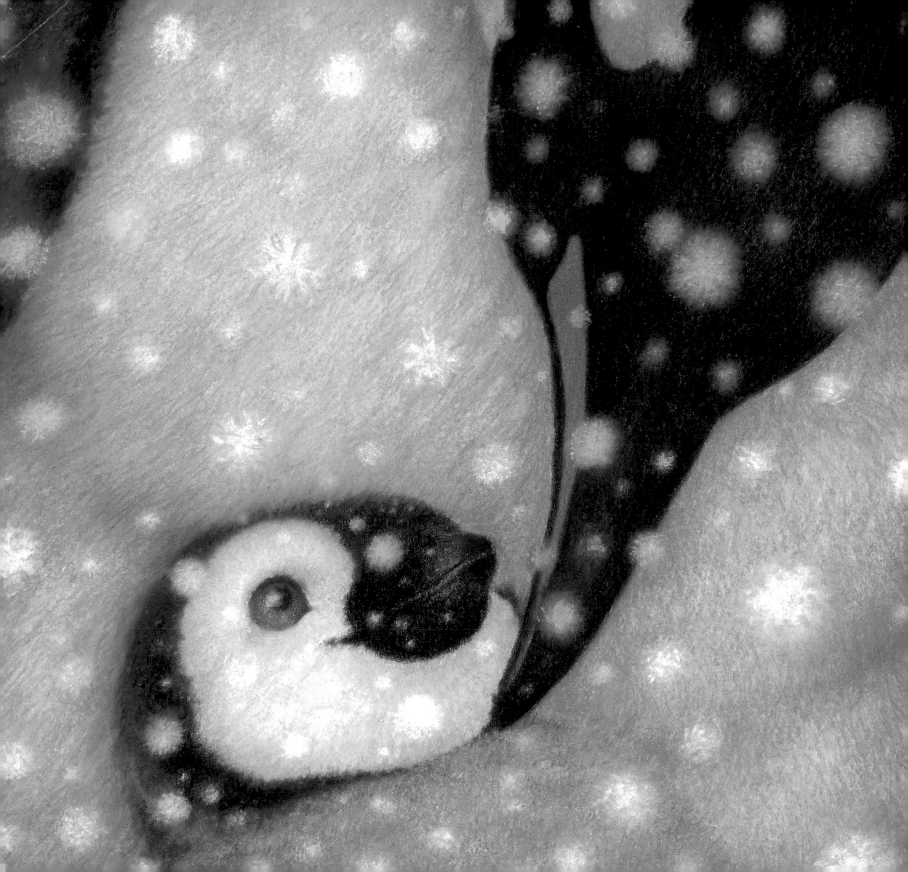

A beak came down and Otto looked into Claudius's face for the first time.

'I'm sorry, Otto,' said Claudius. 'I hadn't realised how grown up you are now. What would you like to know?'

'Why haven't I fallen off?' asked Otto.

'Fallen off what?'

'The world. Leo says we live on the bottom of the world.'

'We do. Antarctica it's called, the South Pole. But you won't fall off.'

'Why not?'

'Because I say so. Now we'd better stop talking and join the others. A blizzard is coming and it's going to be very, very cold.'

Otto wanted to ask what a blizzard was – but he soon found out.
The wind got stronger and colder. Snow was driven at them harder
and harder.

'Otto, come under the feathery flap on my tummy,' said Claudius.
'It will protect you.'

They shuffled across the ice towards the other penguins who were
huddling together to keep warm. Otto had never been so cold.
He thought that the snow and the wind would go on for ever!

'I didn't like that,' said Otto when the wind had died down at last.

'Well – you'll just have to get used to it,' said Claudius.

One day Claudius said,
'You're big enough to walk beside
me now, Otto. Soon you'll have
all the other chicks to play with.'
    'What other chicks?' Otto said.
'There's only Leo and me.'
    But Claudius was right.
Otto and Leo were just the first
chicks to hatch. Now all the
grown-ups were shuffling around
with chicks on their feet.

At first Leo and Otto were the only ones big enough to leave their fathers' feet to play. One of the new chicks wanted to join in but he was too little.

'What's your name?' Otto called.

'Gusto,' the little chick called back. 'Can I play with you next time?'

'When you're big enough,' Otto replied.

'I'm not very big outside, but I'm *enormous* inside,' said Gusto.

'You're going to have trouble with that one,' laughed Claudius.

'Why?' asked Otto.

'You're first chick,' Claudius explained. 'It's your job to look after the others.'

It was true. The very little ones didn't understand that they must stay together to be safe and Otto had to keep rounding them up.

'Come back!' he yelled. 'I'm first chick and you must stay close to me.'

'Oh, you are bossy, Otto,' grumbled Gusto.

The next morning, Otto called
up to Claudius,
   'I have an asking sort of feeling
in my tummy. What is it?'
   'You're hungry,' replied Claudius.
   'Let's go and see if the ladies are
back from the sea.'
   'The ladies?'
   'Yes, they've been eating fish and
things so that they can feed you
and the other chicks. I'm hungry
too, Otto. I shall have to say
goodbye and go off to the sea to
find some food. I've had nothing
to eat all winter.'
Otto was horrified.
   'Don't leave me,
Claudius. I need you!'
   'You'll be fine.
Don't worry. I'll find
a nice aunty to
look after you.'

Otto had never been away from the rookery of penguins before.

'The bottom of the world is very big,' he whispered.

'Look, Otto,' said Claudius. 'Here's Anna. She'll be a good aunty for you.'

'I don't want an aunty,' said Otto. 'I want you.'
Claudius rubbed the top of Otto's head with his beak.

'I'm sorry, ' he said. 'But emperor penguins have to get used to lots of different mothers and fathers when they're growing up. We look after each other. Can you look after me?'

'How?'

'My asking feeling inside really hurts,' said Claudius.

'You can help me by letting me go.'

Otto knew what he had to do. He waddled round to Anna.

'He's our first chick this year,' said Claudius.

'I shall be very proud to be his aunty then,' said Anna.

'Open your beak and I'll give you some fish soup.'
In a few minutes the asking feeling in Otto's tummy had gone.
But so had Claudius.

Luckily, Otto was so busy during the next few days that he didn't have time to miss Claudius. As the ladies came back from the sea, all the fathers disappeared one by one to feed themselves. Otto had to look after the chicks.

When they began to get cold Otto and Leo collected them into a tight huddle, but one chick stood all by himself, looking out to sea.

It was Alex, the last chick to hatch. Otto knew he must get him into the huddle quickly.

'Where's Daddy?' wailed Alex, as soon as Otto reached him.

'I expect he was hungry,' Otto said. 'Stay close to me and I'll look after you. That's what emperor penguins do. They look after each other.'

Otto tried to push Alex into the middle of the huddle but he wouldn't move.

'I want to stay with you,' he said.

'Old bossy chick has a baby!' laughed Gusto.

'Alex, this is Gusto,' said Otto. 'He talks a lot.'

'Can you tell stories?' asked Alex. 'I like stories.'

'Where do I get a story from?' asked Gusto.

'Out of your head,' said Otto. 'Start with "once upon a time" and just carry on.'

So that's what Gusto did. Soon little Alex was so happy listening to the story that he forgot how cold he was.

Later they went to find Aunty Anna.

'Two chicks to feed?' she said.

'I'll have to go back to the sea again.'

'Does that mean I'll have to get used to somebody different?' asked Otto.

'Yes,' said Anna kindly. 'But that's what we penguins do.'

'I'll get used to it,' said Otto bravely.

As it turned out, Otto enjoyed meeting all the different grown-ups, especially Justin. He asked him all the questions that he would have liked to ask Claudius. In fact, he asked so many questions that sometimes Justin felt tired.

'Just one more question for today,' said Justin.

'When can I toboggan?' Otto asked. 'I've seen the grown-ups slide across the ice on their tummies. It looks fun.'

'You'll be able to toboggan when you have your adult feathers,' Justin said.

'When will that be?'

'That's two questions,' Justin smiled. He moved away, but he called back over his shoulder, 'Soon.'

A few days later the cold wind began to blow and Otto knew he had to get the smaller chicks into a huddle. It was easier now there was Gusto to tell stories.

Little Alex crept up to Otto after the huddle.

'Otto,' he said. 'I think I'd better tell you something. You're going bald!' Otto looked at his tummy. There were patches of down missing and thick white feathers showing through underneath.

'Yippee!' he shouted.

'Don't you mind?' said Alex.

'Mind?' said Otto. 'Going bald means I'm becoming a proper penguin!'

Soon Leo and all the older chicks had bald patches too.
They all wondered what was going to happen next.

It was another first chick who told them. Her name was Josie. Otto met her on the edge of the rookery.

'You've shed all your down,' she said to him. 'That means you're ready.'

'Really?'

Josie waddled all round him. 'Yes. Really. You've got all your adult feathers. Now you're waterproof! What about me?'

Otto waddled round her.

'There's a tiny tuft left on your back. Shall I peck it off?'

'No, it has to come off by itself – when the feathers underneath are oily enough.'

Leo couldn't believe Otto was a proper penguin at last.

'How about me?' he asked.

'You have two bits of down left on your back.'

'Oh, please peck them off,' Leo begged.

'No,' Otto said. 'You must wait.' Leo groaned.

'We're always waiting for something.'

'Yes,' grinned Otto. 'I'm having to wait for *you* before we go to the sea. But don't worry. I'm not going without you.'

The next day, none of the grown-ups would
feed Otto or the other young penguins.
'You're not chicks any more,' they said.
'What do we do now?' Leo wailed. 'We're starving.'
'What do you think we do?' said Otto. 'Where can we find fish
and squid and all the things the grown-ups keep bringing us?'
'The sea!' Leo said and he started to waddle off.
Otto shot past him.
'Toboggan!' he cried. 'It's quicker. And it's fun!'
Soon he bumped into Josie.
'I've always wanted to do this,' she said.
'Me too,' said Otto. 'But do you think it's all right for us to leave our huddles?'
'They'll be fine,' she said. 'It's warmer now. Come on. I'll beat you to the sea.'

But their jobs as first chicks weren't quite over . . .

When they reached the sea, the
young penguins were afraid to go on.
Otto remembered what Claudius
had said:

'Penguins look after each other.'

'Food!' Otto yelled as he and Josie
splashed in. 'Come on, it's easy!'
The other young penguins jumped
in and began chasing fish and squid.
They weren't hungry for long.

'It's like flying in the sea!'
said Otto excitedly.
Then Josie showed him one last thing.

'It's called penguins' leap,' she said
as Otto torpedoed up and out of the
water as fast as he could, landing on
the cliff next to her. He felt so pleased
with himself. He could toboggan, he
could swim, he could feed himself
and now he could leap.

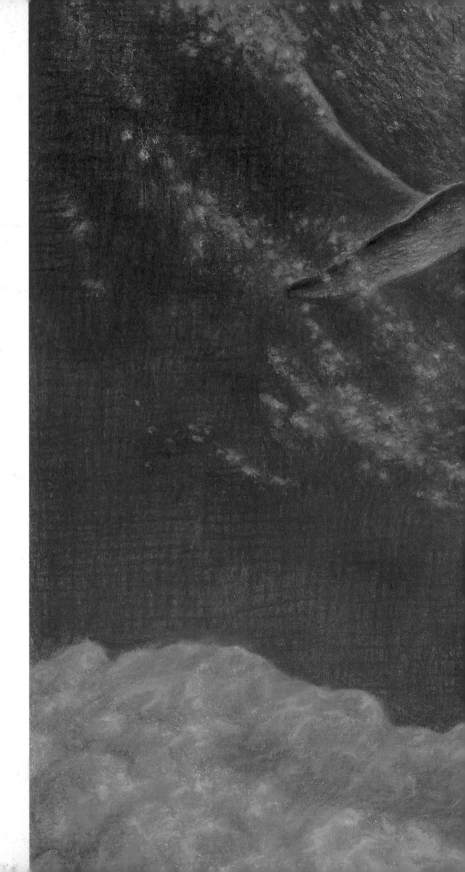

'Well, Otto,' said Josie. 'Do you like being a penguin?'
'I'll get used to it,' he said happily.